Run Fast, Milo!

Written and illustrated by Julie Sola

SPRING HOUSE PRESS

Meet Milo. He wants to go for a walk.

He looks toward the door.

He walks down the hall.

He looks out the window.

He looks out the door.

Come on, let's go for a walk!

They go outside.

Milo passes by his friend Pablo.

He sniffs a bug.

Soon he is at his favorite place!

Once inside, he waits for
his favorite words.

RUN FAST,

MILO!

He takes off running.

He runs past some dogs.

And he runs.

He runs past two children
eating ice cream.

And he runs.

He runs past a little girl with balloons.

Milo stops to get a drink of water.

Milo loves being outdoors.

Then he is off and running again.

He passes a game of frisbee.

Milo makes a great catch!

Soon it is time to go home.

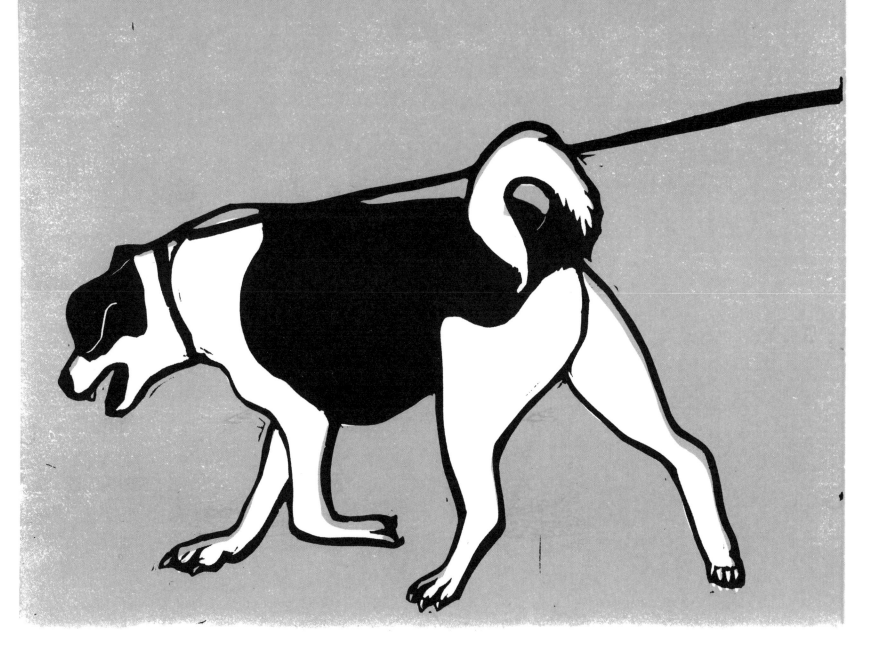

Milo is hungry after his big day.

He eats his dinner.

Milo is sleepy after his meal.

He heads to bed.

Milo falls asleep and dreams about running.

The End.

ABOUT THE AUTHOR

Over the years, Julie Sola has worked in various galleries and schools, teaching and selling art. One stint involved working as a designer and printer at Hatch Show Print, an historic letterpress poster shop in Nashville, Tennessee, that has been in operation since 1879. Her work there involved designing, typesetting, and printing everything from wedding invitations to concert posters. In her off-hours, she began creating her own work and now sells and exhibits at art festivals, galleries, and museums around the country, including the Frist Center for the Visual Arts.

Julie begins with a sketch. Once the drawing is fully developed, she transfers it to linoleum, where the drawing evolves as she carves it. The art is then printed by hand. Her latest collection of this unique hand-printed artwork can be found in *Johnny's Cash & Charley's Pride: Lasting Legends and Untold Adventures in Country Music*.

When not hunched over a block of linoleum or sketching images inspired by her rural upbringing, she tours with various musical acts—including KISS and Rod Stewart—doing costume and wardrobe. Julie lives and works in Nashville, Tennessee.

ABOUT THE ARTWORK

Original hand-pulled linoleum cuts were carved and printed by hand at Hatch Show Print in Nashville, Tennessee, on a 1968 Vandercook proofing press. Any imperfections are part of the beauty of a hand-pulled print.

ABOUT MILO

Milo is Julie's father's dog. Milo loves to go on walks, especially when he is set free to run as fast as his little dog legs will carry him.

Publisher: Paul McGahren
Editorial Director: Matthew Teague

Spring House Press
3613 Brush Hill Court
Nashville, TN 37216
ISBN: 978-1-940611-74-7

Library of Congress Control Number: 2017939856

Printed in China

First Printing: August 2017

To learn more about Spring House Press books, or to find a retailer near you, email info@springhousepress.com or visit us at www.springhousepress.com.